to Cher,
one sweet cookie

I do not like
the look of
that title.

First Edi
10 9 8 7 6 5 4 3

F322-8368-0-11

Printed in the United States of Ame
Reinforced bind

Willems, Mo.
   The duckling gets a cookie!? / words and pictures by Mo Willems. — 1st
      p. cm.
   Summary: Pigeon is very angry when the duckling gets a cookie just by
asking politely.
   ISBN 978-1-4231-5128-9
[1. Pigeons—Fiction. 2. Ducks—Fiction. 3. Cookies—Fiction. 4. Etiquette—
Fiction. 5. Humorous stories.] I. Title.
   PZ7.W65535Du 2012
   [E]—dc23   2011012304

Visit www.hyperionbooksforchildren.com and www.pigeonpresents.c

The Duckling Gets a Cookie!?

words and pictures by mo willems

Hyperion Books for Children
New York
An Imprint of Disney Book Group

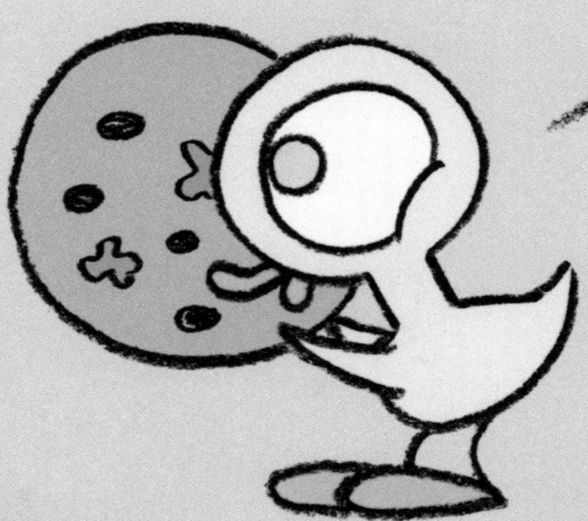
Oh!
Look at all those nuts.

I ask to drive
the bus!

I ask for
hot dog
parties!

Do I ask
for candy?

I do.

It doesn't have
to be a big bus,
y'know....

I'll ask for a French Fry Robot" very now and then.

I've asked for a walrus!

Right now, I'm asking, "Why?"

WHY? WHY? WHY?

Ohhhh... there's more!

Sometimes I ask for a hug.

Or I'll ask for one more story!

I can't count the times I've asked for my own personal iceberg.

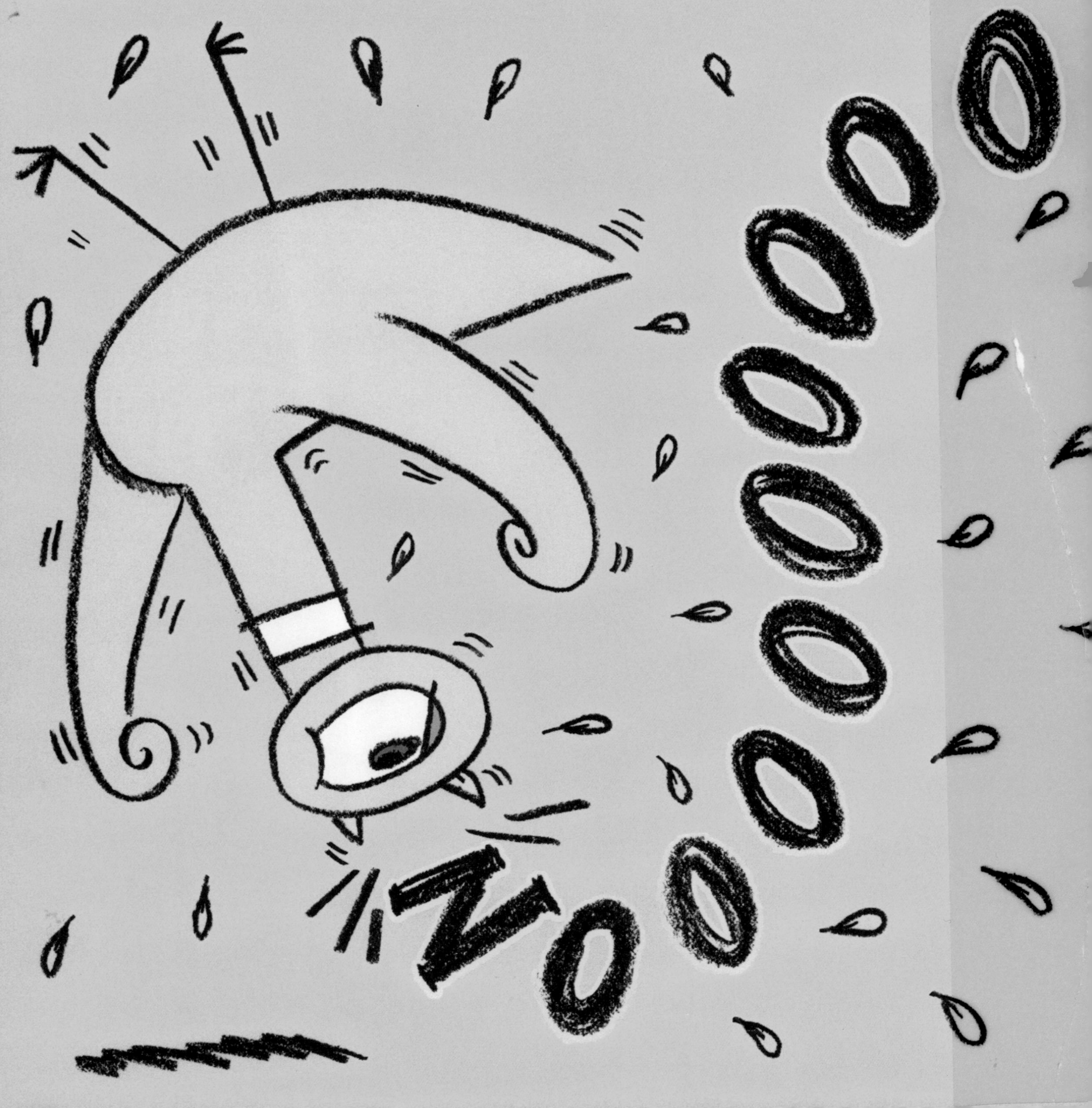
NOOOOOOOOO

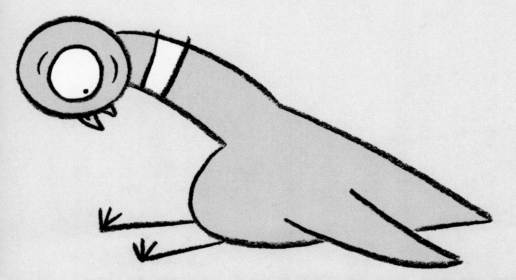

So I could
give it to you.

May I have
another cookie,
please?

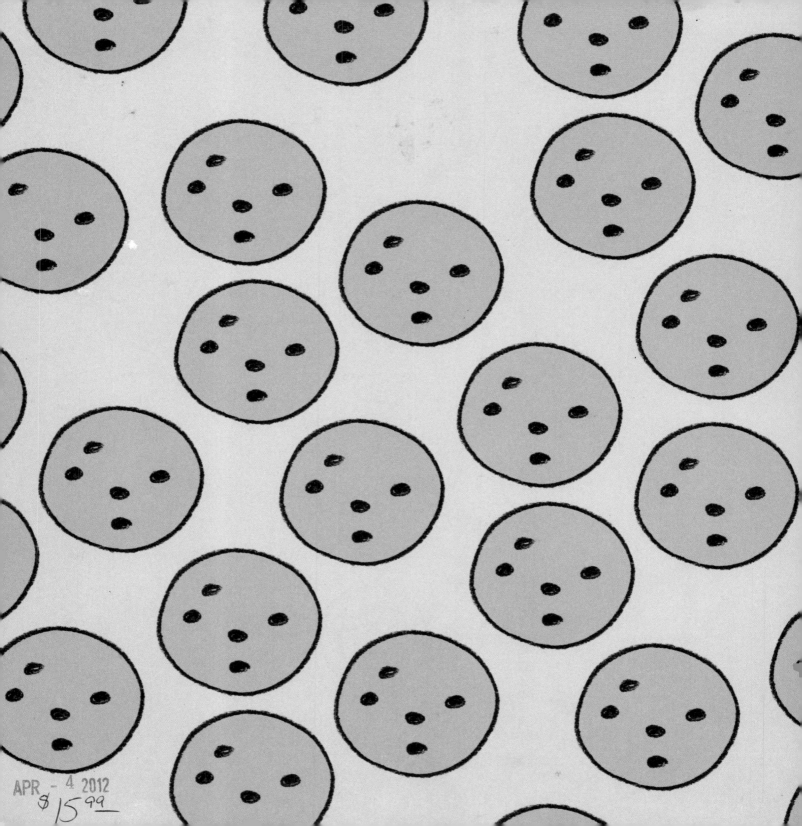